THE ADVENTURES OF
Hamish McMoosie

~

HAMISH McMOOSIE AND THE
MARVELLOUS SET OF NEW BAGPIPES

~

This book belongs to

Dedication

This tale is dedicated to children everywhere

For lovers of the flowing Scottish tune "Westering Home", I am sure that Hamish's rendering of it, played in jig time, would most certainly bring tears to the eyes. We can only conjecture as to the effect of "Westering Home" as played by Sergeant Earnest MacBlast of the Dundee City Mouse Police Pipe Band.

Published 2003 by Waverley Books, David Dale House, New Lanark, ML11 9DJ, Scotland

Copyright © Text – Terry Isaac 2003

Copyright © Illustrations – Mandi Madden 2003

The right of Terry Isaac to be identified as the author of this work has been asserted by him in accordance with the Copyright, Designs and Patents Act 1988

A CIP catalogue record for this book is available from the British Library

ISBN 1 902407 30 X

Printed and bound in Poland

Designed and typeset by twelveotwo

Hamish McMoosie

~

HAMISH M^cMOOSIE AND THE MARVELLOUS SET OF NEW BAGPIPES

~

TERRY ISAAC

ILLUSTRATED BY MANDI MADDEN

WAVERLEY
BOOKS

You may well recall that all was not well in the old city –
even more so in the McMoosie household. Hamish was
still very sad over the tragic loss of his one and only set
of bagpipes. And, as everyone knows, it is a most terrible
thing for a piper who plays in the Keltic Moosie Pipe and
Fiddle Band to be without his pipes. The bagpipes had
become, Aunt Maude had said, "attached to the pointed end
of my long, black umbrella with the goose-head handle".

The result of the accident was that the bagpipes were
broken beyond repair. Hamish comforted himself with the
fact that at least Aunt Maude had now gone back to her
home in Edzell castle and had taken her umbrella with her.

There was only one thing to do, Hamish thought sadly,
and that was to put the pipes away in the store cupboard.
They would never be played again.

Hamish could not bear the thought of
parting with his pipes. This time, instead of
just dropping them on the floor, he gently
wrapped the pipes in tissue paper,
placed them in their special
cardboard box and lifted them
carefully onto the shelf in the
store cupboard.

"If only I had done this
before," Hamish thought to
himself sadly, "my pipes would
not now be broken beyond
repair. My pipes . . .
my pipes . . ."

A big salty tear fell from Hamish's eye and trickled down his cheek. He sniffed and wiped it away quickly with the back of his paw.

Hamish decided that there was only one thing to do and that was to go up into the city and see Alisdare MacBrymer the bagpipe maker. MacBrymer would make him a new set of pipes.

The pipe maker lived under the kindly grocer's shop on David Street, with a collection of hairy Scottish spiders.

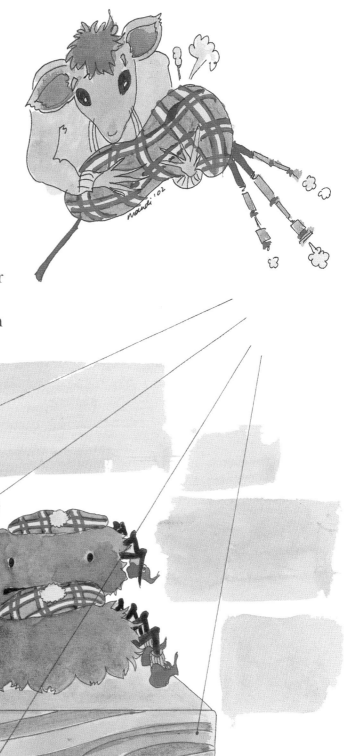

MacBrymer always remarked that it was a very good place for any mouse to live. He had lived under the grocer's shop for longer than any of the mice folk could recall.

Rumour had it that he was probably older than Hamish's Aunt Maude, and as everyone knew, she was very old indeed.

Food was always left out for MacBrymer, especially pieces of fine Arran cheese, by the kindly grocer who was a friend of Bill the gardener. The two friends, gardener and grocer, had an understanding of nature and Moosie things. Once a week the pipe maker had a real blow-out feast when the kindly grocer left out a slice of Arran cheese and a little of the delicious meat loaf that Willie his assistant made every Wednesday. A slice of Willie's meat loaf on a Brechin Heckles biscuit, followed by a smidgen of tangy Arran cheese, washed down with a cup of dandelion tea was pure heaven.

Hamish came into the shop just at the right time. MacBrymer was making his morning cup of tea. Before Hamish had time to say "good morning" the old bagpipe maker looked up from pouring the milk into his cup of tea. He poured a second cup.

"I suspect, Hamish McMoosie, that you have come about a new set o' pipes. I hear tell that yours met with some kind of accident."

Hamish sighed, and picked up the cup of tea that old Alisdare pushed across the workbench towards him.

"No chance of a biscuit to go with the tea, I suppose?"

The biscuits were duly passed over and Hamish selected one of his favourites: a crisp Abernethy. He was about to dip the Abernethy in his cup of tea but thought it would be better not to do so. You see, Abernethies have a habit of breaking up when dunked in tea and would leave a kind of brown, Abernethy sludge at the bottom of the cup. Dorma was always complaining to Hamish that when she came to put the dirty cups in her dishwasher she always found a soggy mess at the bottom of Hamish's mug – leftover Abernethy. Sometimes, when Dorma was looking the other way, or was doing something else about the house, Hamish would stick his long whiskered nose in the cup and lick up the soggy Abernethy with his tongue. He thought that, in this way, Dorma would not know of his habit of dunking. But, typically for Hamish, he always got things wrong. It was a very good plan, to lick up the soggy mess at the bottom of the cup but, unfortunately, small pieces of the soggy Abernethy had a habit of sticking to his whiskers. Although she never said a word, Dorma always saw the wet crumbs sticking to one or more of her husband's twitching whiskers.

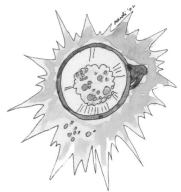

The pace of life for the mice folk of the old city matched the style of the slow country life led by the city's humans. There was always time for a chat – always the time of day to be passed when one went into a shop. There was a need to know who had won what prize in the local flower show, what new shop might be opening on the High Street and, of course, most important to of all the folk, mice and human alike, how did the City football team get on in the last game they played?

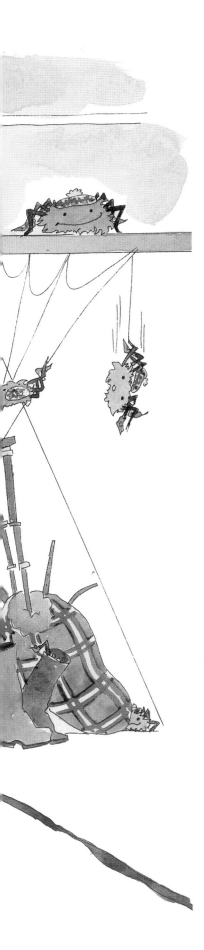

However, and it was a big "however", in Alisdare MacBrymer's bagpipe shop, politics was the subject that had to be aired, before things could be bought. The old bagpipe maker coughed a gentle cough to make sure that he had Hamish's attention.

"I hear that the Scottish Parliament is considering putting a tax on Forfar bridies, and Arbroath smokies."

Old MacBrymer left the words hang in the warm air of his shop and sipped his tea. Hamish, who had just taken a bite of his crisp Abernethy, spluttered.

"Eh? What? Where did you hear that rubbish MacBrymer? They would never dare!"

Hamish waited for an answer. He saw that the pipe maker was slowly dunking his Brechin Heckles biscuit in his cup of tea. Almost right in, Hamish noted. Perhaps Heckles did not break up when dunked. Hamish thought that he might possibly try dunking one of the Brechin-made biscuits later. Normally Hamish spread his Heckles with butter and strawberry jam and did not dunk them in his mug of tea.

"Heard it from my cousin, the pipe maker in Edinburgh, who heard it from a senior civil servant mouse, who overheard it during a meeting with the Moosie Member of Scottish Parliament for the Isle of Mull. Seems that the new parliament building is costing so much money that new taxes might have to be raised to pay for it."

"But bridies, and smokies! No never. It is beyond belief!"

Hamish, who found himself in dire need of another biscuit, having finished his Abernethy, reached over for a Brechin Heckle. As he reached for the tin, the pipe maker snapped the tin lid shut.

"Now what was it that you were wanting Hamish? No time for more tea or biscuits, I have a business to run."

The whole matter of the possible taxes on Forfar bridies and Arbroath smokies was dropped. Hamish, who was not very up on things political, resolved to himself that he would take up the matter with Inky MacWriter the editor of the local paper. He and Hamish often sipped a damson wine together at the Haggis and Neeps Inn. Inky, being the editor of a newspaper, would know, thought Hamish.

Hamish decided to get back to the business of why he had come.

"I want a new set of pipes, please. To replace my old ones, that is."

"By 'new', Hamish, do you mean, 'new' or do you mean 'new to you, but second-hand to me'?"

This question posed by MacBrymer set Hamish a problem. He had not really considered the practicalities of whether to buy a brand new set, which of course would have to be made, or to buy a used set of bagpipes. Then, of course, there was the cost of the pipes to consider. He wished he had an Abernethy biscuit to help him think. Even a Heckles might help his brain work out what to do.

"Well?" asked Alisdare MacBrymer.

Hamish thought. He knew that the Keltic Moosie Pipe and Fiddle band had a wedding engagement at the Northern Hotel the coming Saturday, then there was always the Ceilidh night on Fridays at the Haggis and Neeps Inn. He doubted very much if Alisdare MacBrymer could make a new set in just five days.

"How long will it take to make a brand new set, if I was to order one?"

"I could make you one in about a month. There's a lot to do in the making of a set of pipes Hamish me lad."

A month! That was of no use at all. Hamish let out a sorrowful squeak. "What on earth would the Keltic Moosie Pipe and Fiddle band do without their piper?" Hamish thought frantically.

Hamish jumped up and ran around in circles, filling the shop with his quivering voice. Three of the spiders, who had just finished their morning cups of tea, fell out of their webs and landed in a tangled heap of legs on the top shelf.

"Now stop that running around in circles and squeaking like that. You are giving my spiders a headache."

MacBrymer caught hold of Hamish's kilt, as Hamish ran round him for the fifth time, and hauled him back.

"Thinking of Wailing MacSquawk are we Hamish? He would love to fill your place with the band . . ."

MacBrymer chuckled to himself. He had a liking to tease people in a good-humoured way. MacBrymer really had no time for MacSquawk who was a boastful sort of character. MacSquawk was always telling people that he was the best piper in the county of Angus. Hamish, however, (who really was the county's best piper) never bragged about his ability to play the pipes.

On the top shelf, the spiders – who had now untangled themselves from their collective twenty-four legs – were deep in conversation. They too had heard Wailing MacSquawk play and were in no hurry to repeat the experience!

Hamish admitted to MacBrymer that he was indeed thinking of MacSquawk and was worried that MacSquawk would take his place. A whole month would give that poor excuse for a piper, Wailing MacSquawk just the chance he was looking for to take over Hamish's piping for the Keltic Moosie Pipe and Fiddle Band.

MacBrymer was scratching his whiskers and tapping a foot impatiently, waiting for Hamish to settle down and make up his mind on whether to order a new set of pipes. The old bagpipe maker's eyes strayed to the shelf above his workbench and an idea formed in his mind. The shelf held all sorts of bits and pieces of bagpipes, chanters, flutes, and even a dusty old accordion. As it was rarely used, the spiders had made their webs up there and raised their children in peace. The pipe maker vaguely recalled that somewhere amongst the clutter should be a brown leather bag with the Tayside Mouse Police Crest emblazoned on the outside.

"I can't possibly wait a month for a new set. I just can't!" burst out Hamish at last.

Hamish stood dejectedly, his whiskers drooping, his ears folded over and his long tail curled tight up. Alisdare tut-tutted and coughed a little cough.

"There is a chance that I may be able to help you, Hamish, in the short term that is, and only if you are considering buying a new set of bagpipes. If only I could remember where I put that bag."

"What bag is that?"

"The one I put on the shelf, the one with the Tayside Mouse Police crest emblazoned on it."

Hamish muttered that he could not see how a bag could help with the problem. It was a set of bagpipes he needed, not a bag, even if it did have the Tayside Mouse Police crest emblazoned on it. The pipe maker scratched his whiskers and thought. He knew that he had put the bag somewhere. Then he remembered . . .

"Right, Hamish, there is only one thing to do. It's up on my workbench for you, my lad, and you will have to look on that shelf for me."

Avoiding a sharp pair of tailor's scissors that Alisdare had inadvertently left lying open, Hamish climbed up onto the workbench. The spiders looked down and feared the worst. They were not to be disappointed. Hamish could see all the bits and pieces that cluttered the shelf. Bits of this, bits of that. A tin or two containing who knows what and, at the back, behind a large dented tin of Abernethy biscuits, Hamish saw a dusty, brown leather bag that had a crest on the outside. He reached over and was disappointed to find that the Abernethy biscuit tin was easy to move to one side: it was obviously empty. With one paw he grasped hold of the bag and pulled it to the front of the shelf. Dust flew everywhere. The spiders took refuge in the topmost corner of the highest of their webs. The dust caused Hamish to sneeze and, as he did so, he lost his grip on the bag. The bag fell from the shelf and landed with a thud on the workbench. The spiders fell out of their webs and landed in a tangle once more. They held a hurried, hushed conversation that centred on moving out of the shop to somewhere more peaceful.

Hamish lost his footing and he fell onto the bench too, but he landed on the brown leather bag with the Tayside Mouse Police crest on it. Hamish heard a sort of a wheeze and then a gurgling, soft wail that came from something inside the bag. The spiders began to pack their bags. It was all too much for them, what with falling out of their webs and all the noise and dust!

"Hamish! What have you done? I hope that what is inside that bag has not met with a similar accident to your pipes. Let me see. Move over, move over."

Hamish moved over and rubbed his bottom. He had landed right on the spot where Aunt Maude used to poke him with her long, black umbrella with the goose-head handle. He brushed a spider's web from his left ear. The web got caught up on his paw. As much as he tried to shake it off, it stuck firm. After much wiping of his paw with a duster he found on the bench, the web fell off.

"Double bother!"

"What did you say Hamish? Stop playing with that spider's web and muttering to yourself and come and help me."

Using the duster he had found on the bench, Hamish helped Alisdare MacBrymer to wipe the dust from the bag. When it was clean the pipe maker opened the bag and peered inside. Hamish heard Alisdare muttering to himself, and poked his head inside as well.

"Get your head out of this bag Hamish, you are blocking the light. Ah! Yes, all seems well. Now let's have a look on the workbench."

MacBrymer carefully lifted out a bundle of something
wrapped in an old copy of the *Brechin Advertiser*. The bundle
was solemnly placed on the workbench and the wrapping
unfolded. Hamish's eyes grew wider and wider. His tail,
which had remained curled up since the news that a new set
of bagpipes would take a month to make, sprang straight out.
His whiskers bristled. Lying before him he saw the most
wonderful set of bagpipes.

"Now Hamish, I want you to try these bagpipes out, just
in case your fall damaged them. These pipes are very special."

While Hamish sorted out the chanter and the drones and started to inflate the bag by puffing very gently, MacBrymer went on to explain just why the pipes were so special. He told Hamish, who was only half listening as he was concentrating on inflating the pipe's bag, that the set of pipes had been made by his grandfather for Sergeant Ernest MacBlast, the founder and pipe major of the very first Tayside Mouse Police Pipe Band. Of course at that time it was called the Dundee City Mouse Police Pipe Band, there being no such place in those days as Tayside. Sergeant MacBlast was renowned all over Scotland for his skill with the pipes. His rendering of "Westering Home" played in jig time would bring tears to an audience's eyes. The Sergeant had finally retired and had come to live in the old city. After his death, some twenty years ago, his widow had brought the pipes into the shop to sell. Police widows, MacBrymer explained, did not get much in the way of a pension in those days, and he had given her a good price for the pipes.

Why it must be all of the twenty years since he had set his eyes on the pipes.

"Eh? What's all that? What are you chattering about?" wheezed a red-faced Hamish MacMoosie.

"Oh, nothing – nothing at all. It is just the ramblings of an old man. Now Hamish give us a tune and let's hear how they sound after all this time in that leather bag."

Hamish spread the drones, put the bag under his left arm, placed his claws on the chanter's holes, and played.

A tear formed in the right eye of Alisdare MacBrymer the bagpipe maker as he heard the wonderful sound of "Westering Home", being played in jig time.

MacBrymer said Hamish could borrow the old pipes until his new pipes were ready and that suited Hamish very well. Even though the pipes were old and dusty, when Hamish blew into them, they sang out like new.

The spiders however had made up their minds. After forty years of peaceful living in Alisdare MacBrymer's bagpipe shop they moved out and caught the next bus to Dundee.

Glossary

ceilidh	A Gaelic word (pronounced "kay-lee") for a Scottish party with traditional singing, dancing, folk music, storytelling and fun.
smidgen	A word meaning a small piece of something.
Abernethy biscuit	A traditional and popular Scottish biscuit first made to a recipe of Dr John Abernethy – Hamish's favourite, served dunked in a cup of tea!
Forfar bridies	An oval-shaped, meat-filled pasty rather like a Cornish pasty but without vegetables except for onion. Named after the small town of Forfar but popular all over Scotland.
Arbroath smokies	A type of lightly smoked small haddock with unique flavour. Arbroath is a small town on the east coast of Scotland.
Brechin Heckles biscuit	A semi-sweet biscuit unique to the town of Brechin where Hamish lives, made in the shape of a tool used in the Jute Industry which once flourished in the region. Made by MacKays the Bakers, Brechin. Hamish thinks Heckles are best spread with butter and jam, or with a slice of Willie's meat loaf.

Dorma's Abernethy Biscuits

This recipe has an especially buttery taste which Hamish loves

5 ounces of plain flour
4 ounces of best Scottish butter
3 tablespoons of sugar
1 teaspoon of cream of tartar
Half a teaspoon of bicarbonate of soda
1 tablespoon of milk
1 pinch of salt

Sift the flour, salt, bicarbonate of soda and cream of tartar together. Rub in the butter
to the flour mixture until the mixture looks like bread crumbs. Stir the sugar
into the milk until it dissolves and then add it to the flour and butter mixture.
Form the mixture into a stiff dough. Roll out the biscuit dough on a lightly floured board
to a thickness of about half a centimetre and cut out 10 round shapes with a plain cutter.
Prick each biscuit all over with a fork. Place the biscuits on a greased baking tray.
Bake in a pre-heated oven at 350°F or 180°C for 15 minutes.

Enjoy!

Note: In Dr Abernethy's original 19th century recipe he added Caraway seeds
to the Abernethies which were said to help digestion. If you want to do this
add about half a level teaspoon of caraway seeds to the flour mix.

THE ADVENTURES OF

Hamish McMoosie

Other Titles in This Series

~

HAMISH McMOOSIE AND THE LONG, BLACK UMBRELLA WITH THE GOOSE-HEAD HANDLE

~

HAMISH McMOOSIE AND THE LONG HARD WINTER

~

HAMISH McMOOSIE AND THE QUEST FOR THE NEW SPIRTLE

~